Sephy's Story

Julia Green
Illustrated by Teresa Murfin

A & C Black • London

D1584614

This book can be used in the White Wolves Guided Reading programme
with Year 3 children who have an average level of reading experience

First published 2007 by
A & C Black Publishers Ltd
38 Soho Square, London, W1D 3HB

www.acblack.com

Text copyright © 2007 Julia Green
Illustrations copyright © 2007 Teresa Murfin

The rights of Julia Green and Teresa Murfin to be identified
as author and illustrator of this work respectively have been
asserted by them in accordance with the Copyrights,
Designs and Patents Act 1988.

ISBN 978-0-7136-8212-0

A CIP catalogue for this book is available from the British Library.

This book is produced using paper that is made from wood grown
in managed, sustainable forests. It is natural, renewable and
recyclable. The logging and manufacturing processes conform
to the environmental regulations of the country of origin.

Printed and bound in Great Britain by MPG Books Limited.

Contents

Chapter One

The day started as usual. I played
in the fields while my mother
worked in the vegetable garden –
planting seeds, weeding and
watering the bean plants and
melons.

My mother's name is Demeter.
She is the Goddess of the Harvest.
She looks after the fruit trees and
the olive groves on our sunny
island, too. Growing
things and looking
after them is what
she loves best.

Sometimes I help her.

My name is Persephone, Sephy
for short.

The sun rose higher in the blue sky. It got too hot for running around. I lay on the dry grass and picked daisies. I threaded them into a necklace.

In a minute, I thought, I'll go and find my mother and we can have our lunch under the lemon trees.

We'd made a picnic that morning: fresh cheese and home-baked bread with olives, sweet honey-cake, and a pink pomegranate fruit full of juicy red seeds.

Suddenly, I heard the strangest
sound. It was like the wind at the
start of a terrible storm.

I shivered, even though it
was hot. I stood up to see better.
A cart, pulled by horses, was
speeding over the bumpy ground.

It threw a dark shadow over everything it passed. A man in black urged the horses towards me. Closer, closer they came.

Where could I run? It was too far to the garden or our house or the orchard.

Ice-cold hands grabbed me. I was swept up into the cart. I kicked and struggled but the man gripped me tight with one hand. With the other, he whipped the horses faster.

I screamed.

The leaves on the trees turned red and gold as we passed. They shrivelled and curled up as if they were on fire. I watched in horror as the horses galloped towards the cliff edge.

Then, like magic, the ground seemed to open up. We plunged down, down, down, into darkness.

The last thing I saw was water tumbling over rock. The river!

"Help me!" I called out. I threw my little necklace of flowers onto the water. Perhaps someone would find it. Perhaps my mother would know it was mine and come looking for me. It was my only chance.

"Help me, someone, please!"

Then everything went black.

Chapter Two

I woke, shivering. Where was I? It was so dark, so cold. The air smelled stale and damp. The sound of rushing water echoed around me. It seemed as if I was in a huge underground cave.

My stomach rumbled with hunger. My mouth was dry.

I heard footsteps. My heart beat faster.

A light flickered in the distance. Someone carrying a small rush light was coming along the rocky passage. I watched the shadows dance like ghosts. I trembled with fear.

"Good. You are awake," a man's voice said. "You have slept for a long time. I am so happy you are here. I will bring food and drink. We will celebrate."

The light came closer. I saw the man's face, like a skull. I shuddered.

"Who are you?" I whispered. "What is this place? Why have you brought me here?"

"My name is Pluto," the man said. "I am King of the Underworld, home of the dead.

Welcome to my kingdom,
Persephone." He reached out to
touch my hand.

I shrank back in horror.

"What do
you want?"
I whispered.
"How do
you know
my name?"

"I saw you
playing in the fields," Pluto said.
"I watched you working in the
orchard and the garden with your
mother. She calls you Persephone.
That's how I know your name."

17

I was furious. "You stole me away! How dare you! Take me back immediately! Who do you think you are?"

Pluto looked surprised to hear me speak like that. He stood up straight and tall. "I am a king. A god. I have brought you here to be my wife and make me happy."

He sat down on a rocky ledge. His face was suddenly sad. He spoke again, more softly. "It is dark and lonely here. You are so pretty, so full of life. As soon as I saw you, I knew you could bring light and happiness into my underground kingdom."

"But you didn't ask me what I wanted," I said. "How can I ever be happy here in the cold and darkness, away from everyone I love?"

Pluto looked around the cave. "It does not seem dark to me. Not now you are here," he said.

I started to tremble. "Please let me go," I said. "Take me back home!"

But Pluto had disappeared and I was alone.

Chapter Three

Day turned into night, and night into day. I could not tell which was which. Pluto visited me in the darkness. He talked to me about his underground kingdom.

"I have many treasures," he said. "Gold and silver, and precious stones. There is copper, and rich-red iron."

He lifted the small light to show me the red veins in the rock.

He showed me the shells and bones
of creatures, pressed into stone.

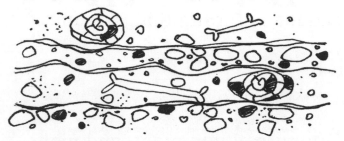

"See this?" he asked. He
pointed to gleaming black bands.
"Leaves and ferns and the relics of
ancient trees have been squashed
down over thousands of years to
make coal. I will share all these
riches with you, Persephone."

"But everything here is dead,"
I said. "They are the ghosts and
shadows of living things. I can
never be happy here."

Pluto brought me tempting
food like sweet almonds and
honey, figs and fresh oranges.
I refused to eat. I would rather
die than eat his food.

The time passed slowly.

I thought about my mother.
I imagined her, searching for me.
She would be missing me so much.

Soon I became weak with hunger and thirst.

"You must eat something," Pluto begged. "Please, Sephy." He held out a heart-shaped pomegranate fruit. He sliced it in half.

I saw the juicy, red seeds. I remembered the picnic my mother and I had made. It seemed so long ago. My mouth began to water.

Pluto picked out twelve ripe seeds for me to eat and placed them in my hand.

I was so hungry! One, two, three... I tasted each sweet seed on my tongue. Four, five...

Suddenly a strange whirring sound, like bird wings, filled the cave. I stopped, listening. I knew the sounds of my underground prison by now. I had never heard anything like this.

"Eat!" ordered Pluto.

I licked the sixth seed.

"STOP!" a voice called out.

I stared in amazement at the
winged creature in front of me.
The remaining six seeds slipped
from my hand.

"I am Hermes, messenger
to Zeus, King of the gods. He
commands you, Pluto, to let
Persephone go!"

"It is too late!" Pluto laughed
cruelly. "She has eaten. She is
mine. Those are the rules agreed
by the gods.

"Anyone who accepts the food I give them in the Underworld must stay with me for ever."

Chapter Four

I stared in horror, first at Hermes, then at Pluto. All my hopes of being rescued trickled away.

"You should've told Persephone before, about the rules. You have tricked her," Hermes said to Pluto. "That's not fair."

Then he turned to me. "What did you eat, Sephy?"

"Six tiny pomegranate seeds," I sobbed. "Such small seeds and only six. I was so hungry.   Please don't make me stay here. I can never love Pluto, never in a million years."

"I'm sorry, Sephy," said Hermes.

"Then why did Zeus send you?" I asked.

"Because of your mother," said Hermes. "When you disappeared, she searched for you everywhere. Finding you was the only thing that mattered to her. She stopped looking after the crops. The flowers and vegetables stopped growing. The leaves on the trees shrivelled and dropped off.

"One morning, as she sat weeping by the river, she saw something floating on the water. It was a little necklace made of daisies. The river whispered its secret, that Pluto had stolen you and trapped you underground.

"Your mother went to ask Zeus for help.

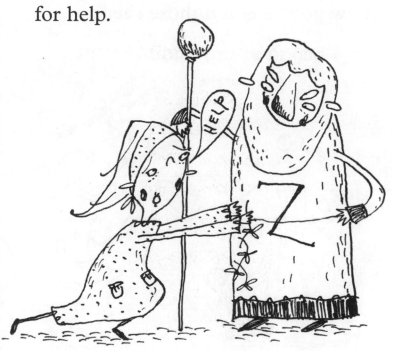

"Zeus knew that if the Goddess of the Harvest stopped looking after the earth, everything would die. So he sent me here to bring you back," Hermes explained.

"I came as fast as I could. But now you've eaten those seeds…"

I began to cry again.

"I will try to help you," said Hermes. "We can't break the rules, but perhaps Zeus will know what to do. I'll come back to tell you what he decides."

"Bring my mother with you!
And hurry, please!" I begged.

I watched Hermes disappear
up the tunnel. But even in the
darkness, I now had hope. My
mother never gave up searching
for me, I thought. And soon I
will see her again.

Pluto sulked and stormed, but I would eat nothing more. I had found new strength. I waited to hear my fate.

Chapter Five

Day after day, I watched and waited. It seemed so long.

At last, I heard the rush of wings and the soft pad of my mother's feet.

"Sephy!" my mother called.

I ran towards her. We hugged each other tight.

Hermes smiled at us. "Now, listen carefully, Persephone," he said. "This is what Zeus has decided."

Pluto came closer to listen, too. I felt his ice-cold hand on my arm.

"You ate six pomegranate seeds," Hermes explained. "So Zeus says you must spend six months of each year with Pluto in the Underworld.

"But for the other six months, you can live with your mother, and help her to care for the trees and flowers and crops, and play with your friends in the fields."

I didn't know whether to laugh or cry. Six months of darkness! But also six months of happiness, in the warm sunlight...

"It will be all right, Sephy,"
my mother said, stroking my hair.
"You'll see."

So this is the new pattern of
my life. I spend six months with
Pluto, in his dark, underground
kingdom.

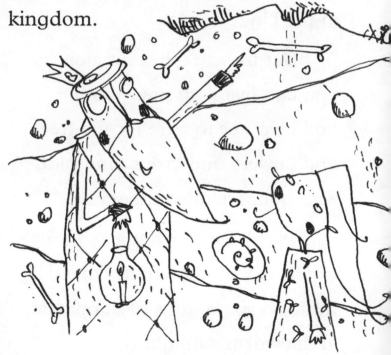

While I am there, my mother is sad and the earth grieves with her. Nothing grows. My mother waits patiently for me.

Now that I know it is only for half the year, I don't mind so much. I sleep a lot. I keep Pluto company.

In the darkness, I tell him
stories about the world of light and
warmth and love. He listens and
smiles. Bit by bit, I think I am
even beginning to care for him.
I understand how lonely he is.
It is not his fault that he was
made King of the Underworld,
after all.

When my six dark months
are over, I creep back up the long
tunnels, up towards light and
warmth again.

Round and up I go,
through the layers of rock
and soil, through the black

bands of coal, and the paler
strips of chalk and limestone,
sand and clay, past the deep
roots of trees.

With each step, I feel happiness creep back along my veins. My heart flutters like a bird.

At last, I push up through the peaty soil, up into the pale sunlight of spring. Life can begin again.

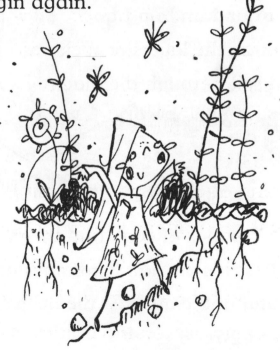

About the Author

Julia Green writes mainly for young adults. *Blue Moon*, *Baby Blue* and *Hunter's Heart* are all published by Puffin. She lives in Bath with her two teenage children and lectures in creative writing at Bath Spa University. She is programme leader for the MA in Writing for Young People. She also runs writing workshops for young people and adults.

Other White Wolves Myths and Legends...

PANDORA'S BOX

Rose Impey

When the world was new, Prometheus made Man out of clay and gave him life. But then he stole fire from the gods and made Zeus angry. The Top God was determined to have his revenge and make Man suffer. So he gave him Woman, who was perfect in every way, except one . . .

Pandora's Box is a modern retelling of the classic Greek myth.

ISBN: 9 780 7136 8420 9 £4.99

Other White Wolves Myths and Legends...

Wings of Icarus

Jenny Oldfield

Daedalus and Icarus are trapped.
King Minos is holding them prisoner
on the island of Crete, where Icarus
can only dream of what lies beyond the
sparkling Aegean Sea. Daedalus hates
seeing his son so miserable. So the
inventor comes up with a plan to
escape, either one way, or another...

Wings of Icarus is a modern retelling
of the classic Greek myth.

ISBN: 9 780 7136 8419 3 £4.99

Year 3

Stories with Familiar Settings

Detective Dan • Vivian French

Buffalo Bert • Michaela Morgan

Treasure at the Boot-fair • Chris Powling

Mystery and Adventure Stories

Scratch and Sniff • Margaret Ryan

The Thing in the Basement • Michaela Morgan

On the Ghost Trail • Chris Powling

Myths and Legends

Pandora's Box • Rose Impey

Sephy's Story • Julia Green

Wings of Icarus • Jenny Oldfield